Urban VerboCity

Poems and Short Stories
by
Charles Pernell

DEDICATION

To my children, Jasmine, Ray, Raegan,
Riley and Sophia and to my wife and muse, Allida
To my parents, Juanita and Charles, Sr.
And to my guardian angels, Walter and Mattie Hill.

CONTENTS

ACKNOWLEDGMENTS

Special thanks to Ti Kendrick Hall for the tremendous book cover and the constant urging and encouragement to write, write, WRITE! Special shout out to Stephanie Renee for showcasing my spoken word gifts at her venues many moons ago at the height of Philly's neo-soul scene. To Art D. Williams for his book layout assistance. And to Daniel Nester whose expertise and appreciation of my style made for a wonderful editing partnership.

INTRODUCTION

Urban VerboCity is a chapbook and first installment of the Joy Chant Series. It is a collection of poetry and short stories based on Dewey and Fawn, demi-gods who live in a place known as Mystical Brooklyn. Mystical Brooklyn is an amalgamation of fifth- and sixth-dimensional abstracts of several urban areas throughout the world. Although the neighborhood may appear to be Crown Heights, Brooklyn, it really co-exists on several cosmic planes at once. Familiar cross streets from different cities intersect.

The book is split up into themed chapters in order to follow the flow of the poetry and Dewey and Fawn.

CHAPTER 1
BROWNSTONE BEGINNINGS

Urban VerboCity!
Before Mystical Brooklyn, there was an Eden
Circa 1925 A.D.

Quiet is foreign to
Urban life here...

Ms. Mattie called her
kids to eat but they were
up the street being
verbose about somebody's
mom on the farewell program
knowing damn well the government
cheese block they lived on was
nothing more than a project.

Cracks in sidewalks
were smoked up by geezers
who used to lead revolutions
against the man and
now eat from the hand
of poison pimps feeding
dope to babies and
are verbose about it, too...

Sizzling like Sylvia's soul
could be heard
screaming in the ears
of many on a sweltering
July day when fire plugs
open to take cool shots
at the hot-blooded folk
leaping from steamy Harlem
stoops into streets of verbosity...

Laughter consumes children
who play loudly, shouting
sheer innocence to the to heavens
above brownstone roofs that
try to stifle the joychants
but can't cause babies screams
are just too strong and
God always hears them!!

Wailing sirens wail
bloody murder from
bloody murdering police
who kicked a whale
of a lie after wailing
on my brother's head.
My momma wailed
that day, too.

And gentrification?
Yuppieville in MY Mecca?
Gentrify my ass and give me
a tax base called a job and
I'll urban renew this mutha fucka
my damn self!! Make an alley
historical just because Robert Moses
pissed in it? Well I done pissed in all of them...
Ain't no history to that!

Can't get a job
blowing whistles for A-ghost train
that don't come through town
no more where no passengers pass
through the door 'cause ain't no
125th Street pride like it used to be when
Marcus and Malcolm strolled...

I remember when...
Langston and Richard wrote
the East and Harlem Rivers,
Verbosity flowed through veins of Mecca
re-birthing me through verbs and nouns
that could teleport Africa
from the east to the West
with the stroke of a pen...

What is Harlem to me?
Africa across the sea...
God's gateway to home
but closed, now we roam
seeking to move through the
spiritless capitalist beasts of
conspicuous consumption that
paw at our every existence....

Takes us home, Harlem...
Take us back the place that
knows no time or space that
reached into our minds and
brought about a time
when serenity was the norm
now noise is the storm
that drenches our thoughts with pain...

And it hurts, sweet Harlem
Missing you and what you were about
makes me scream to the heavens
'cause I know God can always hear me!!

Introduction to Dewey and Fawn "Traffic"

Dewey stood on the corner of a busy Crown Heights intersection and stood static. The world seemed to begin and end at a rapid pace during the course of his existence.

He stood there, reaching his eyesight askance, diagonally, diametrically opposite of Fawn's ass that faced him but he knew it was her. Her ass was his ass and was oh too familiar a lump to be confused.

"Fawn-igga," he bellowed out to the lean, lithe Brooklyn queen who looked every bit the Afro-Puerto Rican she was with a butterscotch epidermis and a head of jet-black silk that grew straight down her artistically arched back but misbehaved in the midst of brownstone reflective heat in July.

Fawn, breathed and stopped. Her head swiveled 83 degrees to the left to catch him out the corner of her eye. She felt his eyes on her ass before she heard his voice and she smiled inside to herself and said, "Yes, Dewey, it's still your ass, papi..."

"I'm coming to you, Fawn!" Dewey made a dash amongst the blaring horns of hacks and transit cops and road warriors that didn't give a fuck about a pedestrian chasing some ass on the other side of the world... or across the street for that matter. But it wasn't just any posterior that roamed Brooklyn that day.

His journey to the other side was met with hostile traffic in the middle but getting to Fawn was more important. She turned and watched the action of Dewey unfold. "Do he know he could get killed?" she thought. She also knew that that was the story of Dewey's life. It drove her passion and made her wet 'cause she knew he was coming for her. She stood on the corner and watched her man come get his ass and she couldn't help but smile.

Unscratched and unscathed, Dewey reached Fawn and placed a raw diamond in her hand that he had mined with his heart and had stolen from a coal truck last winter. He wanted the time to be right to give it her. Everyone else seemed to move like a steady flow of pre-dawn rush hour while Dewey and Fawn had after-life cocktails. She loved her raw diamond aka lump of coal because she knew she had time to love it, pressure it and mold it into a precious gem. She had time with her beautiful ass and Dewey by her side. She only had all of eternity... in Mystical Brooklyn. They are Dewey and Fawn.

Angels Need to Purge, Too: Dewey's Mama, Annabelle

Annabelle sat, strained and focused. Her toes gripped the floor and the balls of her feet helped to balance her while she sat perched on the commode. She was focusing but couldn't relax. Her spirit was constipated. Her love was bottled up because she missed Jimi. He was somewhere, traversing the galaxy and time, playing for crowds of millions. Jimi had groupies but Annabelle had his baby, Dewey.

They met when Annabelle was waitressing at a Jersey Shore diner. He and his band had come in for a late-night meal when he noticed her. His first words to her were, "You're an angel in disguise." Annabelle replied, "How did you know?" A love affair ensued and lead to cohabitation in a loft on the Moon in downtown Copernicus Crater. Dewey was conceived and born some three centuries after heavy dating and, still no marriage. Jimi had commitment issues.

She continued to strain and release. She whispered out in meditation to the god Mudbuttakhan of Fecalfoulapolis to help her move her bowels, but no response. Annabelle calmed herself. She felt anxiety coming on and took a deep breath. She called out to her adolescent son.

"Dewey! Dewey Lovestrong! Please come to the door," she hollered out. "Dewey, play for mommy. Play your violin. It soothes mommy."

Dewey was a wiry six-foot, thirteen year-*oldish* kid who favored his daddy a lot. Although he had an athletic build, he had little interests in sports. He was a musician and wordsmith. His violin was his magic and could literally move mountains with the string vibrations he stroked. He leaned aside the bathroom door jam, peered over at Annabelle and smiled.

"Play for me, son. Please," Annabelle whimpered. She was clearly defeated.

Dewey placed the violin under his chin and proceeded to strum *A Love Supreme – Pursuance* with the expert precision and speed of Coltrane's horn. His strokes were like wildfire creating a massive energy force that resonated though out the house.

"Yes, *YESSSS!*" Annabelle screamed out in an almost orgasmic pitch of relief. The deed had been done. *Plop! Plop!* and then multiple *plops* into the toilet.

Dewey was pleased that he helped mommy purge. He pinched his nose with one hand and waved to her with the other. As Anabelle's head slowly dropped in relief, Dewey came back to the door and said, "Momma, a little less wine and more water. I think you may be dehydrated."

"Get the hell outta here, boy!," she laughed.

A Crown Heights Memoir
Circa Summer 2001

You remember having salmon cakes and grits on a sultry August morning? About 83 degrees, humid and dripping from overactive glands and reactive hormones that only apple strawberry breakfast juice could simmer...but not extinguish.

So we talk about Janet's fake-ass nose, why the Tribe broke up, and whether deeds of a Bush and Dick will continue to fucks us all... yeah...

With Gil Scott testifying and Jill Scott electrifying the intellects taking us beyond your second-floor cozy surroundings... you know the one with the view of the summer storm puddle reflecting pool on the black top roof outside your fourth-floor living room window?

Can you see yourself in that pool? Can you see how the shimmy shines like your smile when I kiss your forehead delicately but hard enough to impress the fact that I am loving you...

"Is it the way... you love... me, *bay-bay*..."

Brooklyn hazy sunshine beats upon the natives who laze on the stoop down the stairs form our heaven. They lie there unknowing of the joys that you bring me with your royally supreme self... truly a jewel in the Crown.

I can remember lying there and staring at your ceiling fan conjuring images of a rickety 8 millimeter movie that started Dorothy and Belafonte in an intimate room...loving... very much like this... you feeling me?

Feeling me like you know me. Leaving me feeing familiar with your finger-popping massages that you administered to me when my kingdom was your *queendom* at the corner of Bedford Ave and Eden, when we danced in delicious waterfalls and cleansed ourselves of every other person on this Earth, including all of Kings County for that matter...

And when you ventured down Atlantic 'cross Flatbush, heading into downtown, the grassroots genuflect to your every…STEP….STEP…STEP.

The native spirits were carefully choreographed and bouncing about you with excitement and honor just to be in your presence.

Yes… you are truly a jewel in the Crown.

I'm feeling you from head to toe, ankhs, Africa and stiletto heels that appeal to my goddess-identified image of you, Fawn, that is all Franklin… Avenue… Diva!

Sixth Dimension Minstrel Street Performance with Dewey and Fawn

Scalp-pulling was Fawn's favorite pastime and she would commence on Dewey's head as he practiced beatbox and rhymes on the sooty brownstone stoop beneath the hazy Brooklyn sunshine.

Braids paraded down Dewey's collarbone long enough for any sister with tracks to be envious of the dope rope of hair that Fawn pulled and spun from his scalp.

Smiles... all smiles from soul mates of neighboring states... she was from "Philly" in this life and he was from Jersey this time around.

But both molecularly transported to this strange land known as Kings County.

And they were stuck in summer-time purgatory and this is only part of their story.

I digress... let me tell you a little of the rest...

When Dewey spit a flow of nouns, adjectives and verbs, his gift of musical words that made him Orpheus incarnate, he would rip and rhyme to help raise the morning sunshine and serenade daytime to sleep with dusky talk.

Enter Neighborhood Whack Ho Poetess (the N.W.H.P), Synquetta Meadows. Now Synquetta was gifted and unique and, at one time, had mortals kissing her feet but vanity fucked her up. She was addicted to her own whackness... smoking her own ego, sipping her own powdered fruit juice, often referring to herself as the Original Lady Marmalade. A loony tune with no room for improvement because she had all the moves according to her. Synquetta busted out in spontaneous song and beats on the street to an unsolicited, disinterested audience.

Dewey and Fawn were no different. They didn't really want to hear her shit nevertheless, they were amused by the anti-muse.

"Fawn and Dewey! Welcome to my show. I am tired. My energy is low. I am supposed to be in the studio, you know! You know I *really* didn't want to perform... I just wanted to observe and "dis" but I couldn't resist being called in front of you all seated on this stoop... I see a couple of new faces on this stoop and I see a couple that I already know... hey, Fawn girl!"

Synquetta began to elaborate on her status in the lives of Dewey and Fawn. The thing is, they were the only two people on the stoop. They observed and smiled.

Dewey replied, "do your thing, Synquetta Meadows, crazy-ass N.W.H.P. of this here Ghetto!"

Synquetta stood with her hand on her chin, eyes shifting back in forth looking for some instrument to beat. "Ah... the 2-liter Pepsi bottle!" she discovered rolling down the street, possibly running to escape being part of her skit.

"Badu stole from me," she said. "I was in the studio and she was supposed to be making me a Spam and Swiss cheese because I was hungry and needed energy. But she poisoned me with tofu and couscous. And when I awoke, she had stolen my song!"

Dewey and Fawn nodded in awe and pity. They knew darn well that Synquetta didn't even know the goddess Badu personally let alone provided her with any type of creative inspiration.

Synquetta beat on her bottle like an African drum of some sort but cut the music short because her voice was more important, *"Oooh... yeah...it's time to decide...which way to go...think I made a wrong turn back there somewhere! DIDN'T CHA KNOW? DIDN'T CHA KNOOOWWWW? I tried to run but I lost my way...DID"T CHA KNOW DIDN'T CHA KNOWWWW? I tried to..umm... daaa daa ddaaaa da DAA. DIDN'T CHA KNOW?"*

Dewey and Fawn held one another while on the stoop during Synquetta's song as Dewey mentally rhymed the world into another beautiful sunset. Synquetta's performance kept them grounded and Fawn cherished her raw diamond of coal that much more as this was confirmation that vanity leads to whack addiction, a serious affliction that strikes athletes, entertainers, CEOs, politicians, patricians, artists and, even, part-time deities like Dewey and Fawn. They, sometimes, believed their gifts were greater than its' receivers. Poor Synquetta... *"Didn't SHE know? Didn't SHE KNOW?*

CHAPTER 2
THE PREACHER'S PREY

Where have All the Flowers Gone?

Do you know? I mean, florally speaking...
You reek like sweet *metamorpha* weed on daffodil Sundays
And then, emote love rays photosynthesizing my eyes in sync with
you...
Home grown, fertile and correct, do you object
to my germinating inside your love?
Do you object to my pollinating and replicating
all the way back to the Garden where it all began, dear friend.

And when I say I miss you… I mean MISSING you like a rib,
like part of me has gone astray and
branched out into the rest of Love's Holiday.
So tell me....where have all the flowers gone?

The soil is rich with dry bones of my ancestral descendants who
Are the protectors of my sorry spirit.
They watch… they listen…they get a feel for things
That make you and me "us"

"Us" "We", extremely selfish statements considering that
the world exist as it does due to what WE did. It is our matrix,
our purgatory while we move in and out, looping through history
as needling specters/spectators.

There's nothing linear about our devotion

It's sporadic, the after is before
Over and over and over...

I ask you, dear friend...Where have all the flowers gone?

Damn...

I couldn't believe you had the audacity
To lustfully lie down with the serpent
Just because I greedily drank from his
Carnally delicious bowl of fire
Swishing the flavor of Mad Sin 20/20
Around in the mouth from which I often
Told the Master, "I love you"

We betrayed His paradise...

Now look at us...
Banished, disenfranchised
Screwing indiscriminately, deceiving under duress
Cain keeps putting that bullet in Abel's ass

Ain't it a trip how the ripe blood of
Yours truly, drips to the ground
Making it fertile for seeds to sprout
Into Babes of revolution

And... you, too, will blossom...
You will also grow into your rightful
Place as Empress of the Heavens
Perfumed of sweet metamorpha weed
Blowing full bloom into
Daffodil Sundays...

Junkyard Jinx: the Purgatory of Dewey and Fawn

"Be still my beating heart, dear Dewey Armstrong! You shall be missed!" Fawn eulogized in a solemn tone while Dewey lied in state in an old fashion bathtub in the junkyard behind the old school. His hands were crossed over the center of his chest with artificially suspended breath and minimal rapid eye movement under his lids. His lips were drawn tightly simulating a stitched effect. His going home gear of choice was a fleece hoodie, a pair of baggy, saggy carpenter jeans and his ubiquitous, scuffed Tims that had literally been to Mars with him and back. Occasionally, Dewey and Fawn's boredom with life led them to playing dead when the seasons changed and the winds, snows, rains and fire cleansed quarterly pains that they felt from the rest of the world. Living forever and on and on in a territorial purgatory was sometimes like Hell except the lattes from the Starbucks there were really good.

Fawn and Dewey were best friends, playmates that double-dutched their souls, intertwined their minds with grand goals of moving humanity to the brink of ultimate love, peace, even nirvana.

The stale autumn breeze browned the once-lusty leaves made them brittle and aged. They hit the ground with a fate sealed by little feet stomping on them while making that potato chip crunch sound. Crisp like snapping brittle bones that were once vibrant and green with roots of life. Sort of like how we do the old folks for real. The maddening sounds of snapping brittle bones reminds us all that life is only four seasons long, one of which you die and the other you slumber in suspended animation, hibernating at least until it's time to cocoon.

Fawn and Dewey constantly relived this shit. Stuck in a "Groundhog's Day" where they never saw their own shadows because God made it so. They weren't allowed to die since they got kicked off the block on Eden Avenue for fucking with Steely McCracken. Steely was that cat that peed on the alter on Easter Sunday and told everyone to line up two by two because his piss was God flooding the world. He told the clergy it was OK to rape little boys. "Them little dudes have it coming when they are walking down the street dressed all provocatively wearing jeans, a jacket and sneaks," Steely said. "What priest in their right mind wouldn't be turned on?"

He was such a devil, that Steely. And Fawn had the nerve to bum a cigarette off this dude because she said she was "curious" about inhaling fire. Wrong move. And then came dumb-ass Dewey, "Puff puff, pass the fag," he clowned and laughed but they knew God told them "don't mess with Steely McCracken."

And now Dewey and Fawn sought redemption not to mention their own peace of existence. He spends the days rhyming down the sunshine and she spends her days loving him a racing time around the world. God told them not to mess with Steely, though. Dewey thinks about that every time he lies in that bathtub. So does Fawn since they alternate. Sometimes, they just want to die.

DEWEY'S RANT, CHANT and PRAYER for
THE NOW-A-LATER REPUBLIC

When we run rampant through
Jungles like panthers through
Courthouses, it brings to mind that
Romantic table Fidel and Che' set...
A bay of pickled pig's feet sounded
Tasty to most hotel guests
Until the stench of insurrection
Spoiled their appetites

And that sexy way we combined
Revolution with passion brought
On visions of Eldridge CLEAVAGE
Or da bomb titz that we
Suckled for sustenance in the dark times
During the explosive silence
Of exploding gun fire and exploding
Cigars in asinine assassination
Attempts/successes on neo-liberators

The glass of the church
Was stained not by the blood
Of rebels or imperialists but by
The people who fell under the
Tyranny of a Now-a-Later Republic
Set up by neo-colonialists
From city hall to suburban malls
Where the children are captured by candy store
Dreams and suffer from decadent decay
After biting unto flavorful false hopes
That somebody actually gives a fuck...

The Infidels... the Evildoers...

When the children are held hostage
In North American ghettos, tropical island
Country sides or Fallujah slums,

Will God make a way for god-less states, Mecca and
Capitalist Patriots to share the bountiful plate
With His Black, Afro, Latino, negro, Americo,
Chicano, mulatto, mestizo, octoroon, quadroon,
honey-dipped, chocolate chip
transfigured mosaic?

Let freedom ring cause we've found the WMDs!!!

Weeping Mothers Dying at the sight of
Uday and a gang of Yankee bullies that shall remain nameless
and shameless making their own rules
On who should live or die in the Now-A-Later Republic...

I missed the Geneva Convention.
Was it in Atlantic City or Baghdad?

The Infidels... The Evildoers...

Let freedom ring from
Martin Luther King Boulevard
To Martin Luther King Avenue
From Martin Luther King Gardens
To Martin Luther King Homes...
because every neo-colony's got
a Martin Luther King something...

So will Baghdad...

Let us pray...

Dear God Almighty
Allah, the Beneficent, the Merciful
Jehovah, the Most High
Buddha
Ornate Golden Pig that sits on Auntie Laverne's coffee table
Grandmom's pictured plate of JFK above the pictures of Jesus and
Martin
sitting at JFK's left and right hands... the holy trinity...

Mighty, Mighty American Dollar...
Dear... ME

I pray to thee for guidance
'cause we can no longer wait
to share that bountiful plate
of spilled blood and human bones
grinded into gelatin to make a mix
called molded freedom...

The Now-A-Later Republic is too sweet to be
Later and we want it now. We want skittles
Dropped from the sky as we sing a freedom
Song by George Clinton, One Nation Under a Groove
And dance in the sunshine of your existence

And I pray to thee to stop the Infidels and Evil Doers,
You know...
Those who are the skewers of YOUR truth
And try to play you on CNN, BBC and Al Jazeera

I pray to thee for a chance at your heaven
if I so choose to believe that...
I pray to thee to come back a more decent and loving being
If I so choose to believe that...

I pray to you now... and forever but never later...

Amen

Gypsy Blue

The Nile supposedly runs through Egypt
But I've seen more history in
Streaming North American puddles
Running down High Street
To meet storm drains at Forever Avenue

The Corner...

Storm drains that catch all the hell
From a collection of crack vials
Shell casings, shitty diapers
And stupid dreams of liberation...

The Corner is a Circus...

Complete with clowns and freaks
Of project mutations of mankind
Brought about from North American
Winters...
Snowing radioactively making
brothers sell blow and
sisters sell blow jobs
It has to be the snow, right?

North American Winters where
Brothers dress in green for the
Frontlines but die for the green
On their front porch when
Vengeful self-destructive
Brothers (i.e. enemies of
The race) place pungently
Sweet black roses on caskets
Open and casting reflections
Of my poor self...

I saw myself in him...

Embalmed and rouged,
Dapper and final...
Making his journey complete
Without reservations or
Ticket the first
And he left without baggage
and his lady...
so then her own issues deepened...

The Corner as Terminus

His woman stood there
Not knowing which direction
To drag those snotty nose
Babies after his reflection
Stopped adorning her mourning...

"Which way? Which way?
She cried out at the corner of
High Street and Forever Avenue

With her feet dangling off the curb
And babies in tow, his woman contemplated
Which way to go...left...right...across
To the other side or she just stay static
Waiting for a ride...waiting to be somebody
Else's woman or a piece in someone else's
Stupid dream of liberation

And...

Caravans of stupid dreams
Ride past in Rimmed-out
Acs and gaudy Cadillacs
Splashing through North
American puddles wetting
Her just enough to catch cold

But she knows no shelter,

Homeless as hell with cardboard
Boxes serving as her luxury
Hotel, her ass even
too dirty to sell because there
ain't no showers at the crossroads
for gypsies.
But a steam vent could be cleansing

The Corner is Cathartic

She submitted. She submitted
Her soul 'cause she remembered
The smile of her sleeping prince
Slumbering under a pile of pungently
Sweet Black roses. She remembered his
Smile and the shadow of his tear-tracked
Face as he lied in state at the Corner.

The steam of submission opened the sister's
Pores allowing all those demons and issues
To dissipate while her man lied in state
at the Corner

Sweet Gypsy Blue found solace
As her own woman
And bathed in the sunlight after
The North American tempest blew away…
Sunlight overpowered teeming towers
And crawling tenements where stupid
Dreams of liberation became her fantastic
Realities …

Jesus Would've Washed Her Feet – Dewey and Fawn

Stripping at the Striped Banana Bass proved to be sometimes a daunting task for Dorothy. Ever since she arrived from Kansas from a tornado and Toto got locked down in the Riker's pound for robbing that liquor "*stow*," Dorothy was lost but her body gave Brooklyn locals pause and she cashed in. She was pimped by this dude name Tinny who had no heart and literally wore bling as his skin pretending to be her friend. He said he would take her to The Wizard so she could get home but she needed some cash. Tinny hung out with this clumsy guy named Crow and some gay cat named Leo who, sometimes nakedly, paraded down the asphalt paved road of Flatbush. Dorothy was lost and turned out... lonely and burned out, and she sought solace in her neighbors.

"Dewey Armstrong, please rhyme me a song to end this long day. Make the sun go down so I can close my eyes to ease the pain away..."

Now although Dewey was a part-time deity, he was a full-time man who smiled and admired Dorothy's cocoa-permanent tan and the shapes that molded the air around her. Dorothy's tight titty tank and boy shorts with ruby-red 6-inch heels made the natives pause, stop, and completely halt at the sight of her country ass.

"I like your shoes, girl!" said Fawn approaching the stoop where Dewey daily rhymed down the sunshine. Dorothy turned and smiled, "Hey Fawn, I like your ass. You KNOW I like your ass." Fawn giggled with her champion strut and slight wiggle and responded, "You like this? Aww... that's nice but it only belongs to papi." Dorothy frowned, "I know, Fawn." She was lonely because she had no one to love or no one to love her. Dewey's daily rap and Fawn's ass and rack were the things that made her smile. She wanted "in" on their action and to be the toy of their satisfaction because she knew they were LOVE.

Fawn put her arm around her and comforted, "You know we would share but it just wouldn't be fair to all the others who want 'in'. We can't compromise our powers for a few hours of tenderly loved skin." Dorothy ascended the steps of the stoop somehow more saddened feeling once again rejected. She entered the building, running from the remainder of day, securing her own personal darkness.

The shadows dropped into the dark as dusk fell over the castles in the Crown. Dewey hit a lyrical crescendo while Fawn privately climaxed at her man's daily duty. The after stillness in the air was softly interrupted by a sublime loop of Dewey's daddy, Jimi, who continued to whisper about the wind crying Mary and excusing himself while kissing the sky.

Dorothy's Darkness

I talked to the Sky yesterday and asked her why she pissed on my head making it soggy and soaked with acid raindrops that burned like hot pokers through my intellect

And she did not respond...

So I asked this trick just who did she think she was that she could go around and plop her big blue ass atop of me and shit suns and moons to shine and radiate on me without my permission.

Bitch...

That fucking Sky thinks that because she covers my world that she can be my girl but she needs to think twice 'cause this is one mafucka don't want no Sky.

I live in darkness...

I live in the pitched black basement where shadows are scared to exist and devils audition for shit that the evilest muhfuckas wouldn't fuck with.

Cold, dank, damp and stuffy, my space wouldn't welcome Buffy because her little ass would be slain over and over and over again.

I live in darkness...

The deep tunnels of depression... Sullen memories of my daddy showing me how much he loved me by callously beating my ass and my mama pampered me by feeding me broken glass in a bowl Captain Crunch.

You ever swallow a four-inch long shard of glass at ten years old?

I'm still bleeding from the attention I was needing to heal. Damn... I wish I could at least scar but the wound is still fresh and blood filled.

And the Sky is trying to smile on me? What the fuck…?

Go away, you big blue bitch with your whitish cloudy locs that remind me of… grandma. You smile like her, too, but I know you aint her 'cause she left me even after she said she wouldn't. She's a liar just like the rest of them.

But don't feel sorry for my despondency or desperation because my depression is rooted in humanity's hopelessness.

What the fuck you looking at, Sky?

I wish you would get out my eyes and let me die dark with the palm of my right hand pressing on hell's ceiling while pledging my allegiance to the death of your big blue ass.
Will you die when I die, sky? Please? Don't stay around when I die, sky. You need to come with me. Will you die when I die or will you still carry radiance and shine? You look like grandma, sky.

With your big blue… beautiful self.

It's lonely in the dark and your light keeps fucking with me. I just want to sleep a forever slumber and not feel your warmth 'cause it feels like grandma's smile.

I don't want your love, Sky, 'cause I don't deserve it. Happiness has never been an option for my psychotic existence or episodic resistance.

I hate you, Sky, but I think I need help….'cause… I…. can't… cope.

So…

Tell me…

It is it true that when folks die, they soar like a dove to you, Sky, like you're some kind of heaven? Or is that bullshit like everything else I feel about you.

I need to know because if I can kick this depression, we might be able to hook up. I mean… one.

I wonder though.

Was grandma REALLY YOU, my big beautiful Sky?

One Black Man's Menopause

Hot flashes!!!

I'm shedding skin or a cocoon of sorts… unfurling into a most beautiful being beyond any gorgeous man 'cause I got destiny on my side

And please…

Forgive me but I'm in a pissy mood, hormones I think…
But I'm in one of those moods that I'm liable
To say anything to anybody at any given time

Let me put it out there for you…

When I write my name in the snow,
I'm leaving my mark on this world to let folks
Know that Dewey is here to stay

With hot streams of consciousness permeate
Icy hearts with vile, pungent, raw knowledge
That could only leave a stench that is so correct
Your eyes will tear…

You'll cry

You'll cry about how you fell for me hard and left me
Quick when you saw my madness as too much
to handle. My affinity to Coltrane should've tipped you!

You say I may just be hormonal?

Excuse me for kissing your ass too many
Times by saying I love you too much and
Always begging for… another day… to love you?

Another day to…forget you… remove you from my system.
Another day to urinate waste from my soul and

Purge my life of the weakness that can drown
A spirit in its own salts…

I digress and yield to memories

Life flashes!!!

Georgia summers when I was not much more than knee high sipping Grape Nehi Pop trooping around Aunt Carnation's red clay amusement park she called a farm. The rituals of hog slaughters, Brunswick Stew brewed on home-made lava pits provided the backdrop for historical summits of family. Even had this stuff they called corn liquor but for the life of me, I didn't think it tasted anything LIKE corn.

Oh and what about Berkley Street memories of dank alleys where hide and seek was played in and out of abandoned houses; red, white and blue Popsicles, Orange milk crates where we thought we could be like Doc or Ice 'cause Mike was still in high school,
Earth Wind and Fire album covers holding buds of herb to be fired;

Millie Jackson "feeling bitchy" during Saturday morning chores;

Mahalia Jackson swooning to Sunday morning bacon popping before we hit New Mickle Baptist's doors!

And me, chilling, backseat of daddy's money-green '75 El Dawg Convertible with GI Joes and Legos in tow. He was a bad man, my pops, flossin' that whip. Everybody thought he had the Billy Dee charm and good looks but they didn't know. He was much more than that. We're a lot alike, my father and I. He had to find his happiness, too…

And still, I digress…

Relationship Clashes!!!

Talk about stifling my creativity?
Just because sometimes I don't wear my ring, she's rifling through my

things, more like my mind to pick and try to find out whether
Or not my proposed happiness includes her. Hmmm… instead of being my MUSE,
She wants to benefit by being included in MY happiness.

Got my hormones messing with my mind but my mama said it's YOU!
I can't stand you but I love you and I need to purge!

So when I flush out myself to purify my HAPPINESS after
I've been through you, don't be offended. It's just that we all
Have to cleanse from time to time, like being on the a crowded
El, you just need to bathe… you just need to breathe…

I wonder if Baldwin, Hemingway, or Wright went through this to live in passion.
Or do I have to move to Harlem, or Key West or Paris to find my happiness.

It sure as hell ain't in passionless nights of Friends re-runs, dried-out chicken and flannel pajamas. That shit is HOT as HELL!

I DIGRESS!!!

Hot Flashes!!!

My eyes are on fire like Black Jesus AKA Ned the Wino cause the holy water I've been baptized with is 80 proof. My holy water… dulls the sting…kills the pain of mid-life *Negroitis*, kills the pain of…falling on nails of crosses bared by hormonal brothers before me. Bitter wine that they said was Grape Nehi Pop but was holy water pissed in snow and sweetened by an angel's soft flow. And now I see… what it means to DIE slowly but with meaning…

And I don't likening myself to Jesus for real
But I'm starting to understand what it is to die for humanity
Only to be born again for the betterment of the universe…

Can you ride the river? Can you ride the river until the mouth swallows you whole?

When that river dries up, life as we know it ceases but a new beginning is in. HEstops my pain and suffering. He stops my blood from rushing like the river that dries up and LIFE as we know it ceases.

My menopause is complete.

Harvest is Coming: PSALM 151 (prologue) (Tanka)

When kindred spirits
Are collected at harvest,
God plants souls to grow
And babes of revolution
Are born to serve his glory

Harvest is Coming: The Prophecy

When winter cries
Teardrops encapsulate souls
That scream to be freed
From Babylon's scorched acreage

Yet, a child rises from
The ashes naked and innocent
To a new beginning with
A heart in his hand

And a crown on his head…
Behold, the young Dewey
Warrior-like yet adolescent
He kneels to aid the princess.

Beautiful and supple Fawn is…
A sister draped in the colors
Of God's infinite glory
And so the journey begins…

Is Babylon dead? About as
Dead as Chi-Raq or Bed-Stuy
On a hot summer night
Hot as hell but His infinite

Glory is hotter!
Do spirits drown in
winter's tears or burn
with Babylon's fears?

Up in smoke are the hopes
of my lost folks and
I can hear them screaming
Screaming to the skies because

Their spirits were sprayed
With Westicide and they
lie dying in fields of delusion
Raised by God's infinite glory

The boy-king's reign
Gives hope and his sister-queen
Gives love greetings
From the Most High!

Chariots storm to the trumpets'
Blare and all ailing souls
That had previously known despair
Have been purged.

Souls salivate at the thought
Of salvation over incineration
And they purge.
They release. They are released…

And, yes, the children shall lead them.

Harvest is Coming (Haiku)

Harvest time for you
Is revolution for me...
Salvation for us.

CHAPTER 3
Love Starts at the El Stop!

Consumed

I think, therefore I am
Consumed in her flavor
Drunk like a lusty lush craving
The passion of smooth cognac
And soft puffs of BIG smoke
From a smuggled Cuban... Blow...Blow...

I am

Consumed in thoughts of
Consummating my love for her
In loops of a matrimonial matrix
In my mind's eye seeing
So clearly that she is where
I yearn to be...

Consumed

Consumed in my woman's wet fire
Stoking and stroking and she
Smokes and tokes on the smuggled
Cuban...blowing my MIND with
Peculiar lusty multi-bred images of

Indian Summer Shenandoah Valleys,
Sassy Harlem Streets and brilliant
Azure coastlines.
She takes me there…

Therefore

I travel light unlike
Others before me who came in
with too much of their OWN baggage.
My carry-on frees me up to carry
HER…and

I am

Consumed with whether or not
She will always feed me what I need
To exist for I am needing her like
a rib to make me whole. I mean
I'm NOT paranoid or obsessed
but just consumed with
her smooth passion and soft
puffs of BIG smoke that engulf
my spirit and brings me to my knees
when I inhale her

I think, therefore I am
Consumed in her flavor
Drunk like a lusty lush craving
The passion of smooth cognac
And soft puffs of BIG smoke
From a smuggled Cuban

My consumption of her
Lies deeper than her
Dimpled smile that
Holds pools of happiness

And lips that trip across

Mine when words aren't
Needed to convey who we
Are to one another.

You see...

I can't remember NOT
Being consumed in
Her flavor when I swish
That wet fire tasty like
Smooth cognac's passion

Like her heart pumps;
And when it pumps,
It beats for me...

You see...

There's no need for
The KY 'cause she
Blossoms like a butterfly
Dripping every bit
Of re-birth on to my being
She is my renaissance...

She not only bore me
But bore for me, she is
Of me... she is my existence.

Saimese, joined at the loins...

We are Consumed

Consumed with whether or
Not, in the end... in the END
Will we be together?

Or

Do we chalk it up as a Formica memoir
Over a late night Rueben and sobering
Black coffee where the scald burns for
The moment and cools after time?

I am greedy and therefore, I am consumed

With every inch of her deepness and
Kisses of her hotness with thrills
Of her newness yet learning
From her oldness

An old soul I knew from
Long ago that always manifest
Itself in wisps of smoke
From that same tangy Cuban
Keeping me infinitely intoxicated
From frenzied consumption of
This sister's spirit…

Not crazily obsessed for I would never
Hurt her or not weakly addicted 'cause I'm not
Trying to hurt myself.

I'm just consumed…to the 3rd degree, engulfed in "she" and me.

I am consumed, therefore,
I…AM…LOVING…HER!

An Analysis of "Us"
(Mentally looping In A Sentimental Mood)

I think sentimental is the best
Term to describe when I saw you…
It had been what? Seven years?

Seven Years…

I mean
Coltrane actually looped through my
Mind when we embraced
And our hearts collided again

Sentimental

Knowing that we once loved
And never realizing how much
Until now

I Love You

It's a funny thing
'cause if I did it right
I wouldn't have run from you
The first time
But understand, I was really running from me…

Running

And you were constantly
Running through my head
Over the years
In and out of my thoughts
With that tangy smile
That always left me yearning
For a taste…

Yearning

Wanting to hold you again
Charging one another soulfully
Wanting to touch you naughtily
Yearning to exchange energy

Exchanging...

You know like
When we used to exchange hellos
With engaging glances
From across relationships

Engaging...

How can a word that meant "Us"
Never ever pertain to us
And just where did I get off
Loving you and still trying
To hold on to your heart, my beautiful flower...

Do I still have it?
Does it still beat at
my predetermined pace?
Can I hold it and move it about
The sky to
Shine your sun on me?

Illuminate

Brightly bathe me with you, baby
Make me feel good about
Who we were and who we are
...'cause I'm in a
Sentimental Mood...

Can't Trust Dis! A Dewey and Fawn Moment

Fawn didn't trust Dewey. She didn't trust him as far as she could spit him. Although, they were mated souls, best friends, thick as thieves and boon coon aces, she didn't trust him. His charisma was a draw to other females. Not that that was what bothered her. She was well familiar with Dewey's connection to mortal women and how his rhythmic words could virtually snatch the draws of an unsuspecting broad. He had words like that! But that wasn't what bothered Fawn. Fawn was fearful of connection. She was fearful that Dewey would connect to someone else as they had connected.

Now, Dewey was no angel, just a demi-god. And just as any demi-god, coupled with being a male, he had an egomaniacal thirst for attention. His brief marriage to a cold, desolate mortal woman left him hungering for the passion and the wild wet breeze that the opposite sex offered. A breath of fresh air. Although Dewey was and continued to be in love with Fawn, he previously lied to her about a mistress he held while being married to the mortal woman. Fawn never forgot and has suspected a continued connection.

"Do you love her, Dewey? Is she the unfulfilled promise of your existence? I think she is," coyly said Fawn. They were lying in the center of Atlantic Avenue, staring at the stars at 2 A.M.

"Do I love you, Fawn?" Dewey deflected. He didn't want to broach this conversation again. It was recurrent throughout time. Century after century. Millennium after millennium. The mistress was now a tortured soul that once and while called on Dewey's spirited literary spit to wash her own pains away. Dewey had previously obliged but no longer. Fawn had sources to check up on Dewey. She was a resourceful goddess that everyone loved and would do anything for. She even had celestial surveillance set up on Dewey. Fawn's stars watched him and audited his transmissions to the tortured soul mistress. And rightfully so. He wasn't right but he wanted to right it.

"Where do we go from here, Fawn? I've wronged you, I'm sorry and I love you."

Fawn smiled. She loved her quirky deity sidekick and was madly in love with him. They began to reminisce about how they accidentally tipped over Atlantis while playing in the bathtub as children. The Pharcyde's "Back in the Day" sweetly played in the background of this episode of Dewey and Fawn's love. And they loved passionately in the middle of Atlantic Avenue in Brooklyn. Stripping into nothingness amidst the molecules of asphalt under their skins. Midnight traffic mystically passing through their lovemaking as the night-time world continued to move, exhaustingly and slothfully.

Crescendo. Resolution and Psalm. Their lovemaking was complete. They held hands and returned back to their brownstone castle. Kissed and exchanged *I love Us* before each passed into slumber. Fawn lied there for a moment, though. Warm, satisfied from the passionate street tryst and sleepy. She smiled to herself, "I just love Dewey so much but… I still don't trust his ass."

My Masturbation Love Poem

The pitter-patter of the rain splatter on my sill warms my mind of that time I took you under the tree in the midst of autumn in New York and Central Park was that stormy rain forest that Lena alluded to cause the sun was still shining to you and me.

And I straddled you across a fallen oak only to find that your sunshine was wetter than the rain. The joggers and muggers were oblivious to our passion cause loving during autumn in New York, sexiness is always in fashion.

The pitter patter of the rain splatter on my sill also reminds me of tea time during Piccadilly Square lunacy and breakfast in Paris, French-kissing and French-toasting one another with sticky syrup and sticky you-on-me and me-on-you.

I... stroke myself with fantastic thoughts of you and me setting sail for Atlantis to renew our thousand year vows and the thousands of babies we have made together over the ages.

And what are the wages for loving you? Infinite cums on my tummy and chest and stroking deeply and aggressively, north to south, east to west. Some may consider it a sticky mess worthy of police caution tape and chalk outlines but they don't know love.

The pitter-patter of the rain splatter on my sill is sometimes interrupted by your familiar cellular ring and you begin to share with me how wet your sunshine is and how drenched the clitter-clatter leaves your thongs. You share with me about autumn in New York and how you love being my French tart and the fantastic mother of my thousands of babies.

The rhythm of my stroke syncopates with Ella and Louis and culminates in spurts of Dizzy's horn blaring before finding Resolution and Psalm in 'Trane.

The pitter-patter of love's rain splatters infinite cums on my tummy and chest where you normally lay your head to rest after real time loving. This master bathes in your wet sunshine although sometimes in my own mind. Can you hear the rain falling? Pitter-patter... Pitter-patter...

Nipple (inspired by Fawn wearing Dewey's white tank tops)

It's awfully breezy in here isn't it?
I mean, you can feel my hot breath
Cut through the chill of your
Host bosom can't you?

You perk right up when I move
My sweet lips fluently and about
Articulating what you want to feel.

Mmmm… you feel that tingle?
Your disciplined way of responding
To me is quite a turn on… I mean you
Stand so erect, attentive, submissive
To my whispers… "nipple…nipple"

I think it was the god Eros who
Once that the "the nipple is
The center of the *libidoverse…*"
Or was that Peanut from 52nd Street?

Nevertheless, you are the
Gateway to nourishing
life that suckles you for existence…

I mean was Oedipus so
Wrong for being anti-Similac
And pro-you, Nipple?

Yeah, it's a l'il drafty in here.
Nippy even… and you seem
Rather uncomfortable, repressed
Suppressed, oppressed…
So why don't you undress, Nipple?

Let me see that mini
Mountainous range virginal
To my exploration, needing its

Pinnacle peaked by a gifted Climber.

A tale of two titties,
It was the best of times and
It was the naughtiest of times…

Yeah…it IS a bit chilly in here isn't it?

Art Personified

Delicately contoured designs are you
'cause regal hips carry the bass of a native
Bong beat from a place called Home.

An image so overwhelming and
As royal as Queen Nefertiti.

Your sultry lips kissed the world
And gave it life when you licked
The back of Africa and placed it
In the center of the Universe!

Kiss me gently, sweet Fawn, and

Strut about me proudly
Whether your doo is fried and dyed
Or "fro-ed" like Angela's majestic
Black Power Puff for

My heart vibes when
Your soul sounds surround me.
Your walk is rhythmic,
Your every move is melodic,
Creating the icon of 'Trane
Blowing his horn
So smoothly and oh so mellow

Strutting through my life
Proud and powerful
Like Nikki ego tripping about her
Nubian Womanhood!

Sing to me with a creative tongue
Scatting throughout the diaspora
Reminiscent of a glorious
Of a Lady that God
Had blessed as a child for having her own.

Whisper your love to me
Softly, my dear Queen
While I navigate the waters of
Africa-America's Nile from Cairo
To 'Nawlins taking us
Home…

We'll venture through
To the Caribe and stop
In Kingston to get
Your sister before going
Back to Daddy's land!

Love me long, my Queen for
You're a renaissance to my soul
Moving and grooving it to a native bongo beat
From a place called Home!

And when Romare splashed you with
Hot, cold lively textures,
It complicated your aura,
Making it glow with the love and pride
of your people who are the Chosen.

So when it was said of your beauty left
Home to serve Europe,
I didn't worry because
I knew my queen wouldn't abandon her warrior
And you didn't for you were
on the frontline with me.

I will always respect you
For raising my mind
To a level of excellence
Sister, you are the painted picture
Of history and the music orchestrated
From a place called Home.

My Fawn, you are Art Personified!

CHAPTER 4
VERBO CITY LIMITS

Angry, Random 9-11 Conspiracy Spit with Dewey and Fawn

Back in '01, Dewey saw the Towers drop the dawn before "the planes drained their scummy jet fuel into the crude orifice that opened up like a raped and gaped ass of concrete and steel." America had been fucked.

Dewey saw it while perched on his brownstone rooftop and witnessed the long cold winter before the snow of ash fell on Battery Park. Dewey had a feeling that Georgie and Dickie had pulled the trick on unsuspecting, trusting, ignorant souls who think it's alright to live in a country where 16 year olds celebrate half million dollar birthday parties and driver Hummers to the mall. No. I'm NOT talking about the U.A.E.

"Who moved my cheese?" You ask. Your fucking government.

"Your fucking government killed, dealt and free-wheeled the free world for free oil and this sick legacy that leaves thick mossy cum stains of disdain dripping down an ass of concrete and steel.

The extermination of life was viewed as an extermination of maggots and faggots that were acceptable collateral losses in the midst of an empire named Sodom while all the while blaming Sadam's empire."

Dewey continued to spit on this dawn on this morn of betrayal. The sun still had to rise and that was his job.

The Nation of B.O.O.S.H. (Brotherhood of an Opulent Societal

Hierarchy) was formed by Dewey in 2nd Century B.C. in anticipation of Tri-Lats and New World Order riff raff. The Intellect Cartel serves as the library of truth and knowledge to B.O.O.S.H. charter membership which has boasted Nat Turner, Garvey, Ghandi, Che' just to name a few.

But where was B.O.O.S.H. on the morning of September 11, 2001? Why did Air Force One rise before the sun and it's precious passenger sat in front of the babies, stoic, unconcerned and undefined for that brief moment of history and time?

Dewey rocked back and forth perched staring squarely at the skyline and tears dribbled down each cheek and connected at the cleft of his chin. He could hear the screams of the soon-to-be-dead in Manhattan and 300 miles south in D.C and points southwesterly in PA. Screams of those who weren't supposed to die at this time but deals were made with a clever devil named Steely McCracken, Dewey's nemesis.

Conspiracy reigned and tyranny shamed the beautiful skies Dewey's ancestors had created. A New World Order that would prostitute its' own daughter for the sick folly of controlling and molding history for the preservation of man's vanity and ego.

Fawn lied in bed that morning, at 5 AM to be exact, knowing that her man was perched atop the roof sobbing. She rubbed his place on the bed and held his pillow between her legs and sighed.

"Dewey Armstrong, it won't be long before the dawn comes and Steely may have won this one. Didn't America bring it on itself? I mean... do our children really need half million dollar birthday parties?"

It was so easy for Steely to influence those planes on September 11, 2001. How much did/do we really give a fuck? Do we? DEWEY?

Another Baby Silenced! (for Marcus Yates)

CRACK!
   CRACK!

Through the still air the shots rang.
In their path was a little boy, no longer will he laugh or sing.

A brother dealing death but not through some deadly drug,
Instead, through the head of the little boy with a .45 caliber slug.

Arrested and incarcerated with bail set at an all-time low,
And to think the judge was surprised when in court the brother didn't show.

A sad commentary as the babies prematurely go to Heaven,
All because lawmakers choose to play Elmer Fudd with an AK 47.

An Introduction to Detectives Epidural and Petalstool
in Mystical Brooklyn

Teaberry got murdered sometime on Friday night and they found him in the driver's seat of his Lex, with a hole in the head and pro basketball playoff tickets stuffed in his mouth. The car was in an alley off of Slauson Avenue and North Broad Street. The gumshoes were on the job though.

Detectives Petalstool and Epidural were old "G" in the Metro P.D. From their start as beat cops some 20 years ago, they continued to cantankerously dabble in interpretation and deliberation of justice in the streets against street justice just because they could.

Julius Epidural was a Mystical Brooklyn native who never vacated the place and placated and pacified the other natives with promises of "niggas goin' down" and "anti-riot" rhetoric in the often crime-ridden streets of his home.

Sayzar Petalstool was a lot less diplomatic than Detective Epidural. Sayzar was adamantly defiant toward the politico that legislated the rights for the societal crumbs that fell off the diseased cake that was Mystical Brooklyn proper. Bureaucracy versus results. The age old argument. But back to the question at hand. Who Killed Teaberry?

Word on the street had it that Shitake Bukkake put a hit on Teaberry because he took extra time and extra liberties from her very special pleasure consultants known as the Mushroom Girls. There wasn't much teeth to that theory. Old Lady Shitake was 800 years old and didn't run as nearly a tight shop as she would have 200 years before. And trooping with Mushroom Girls wasn't really Teaberry style. He never had to pay for the pleasures.

The investigation was on and Petalstool and Epidural came through our block bold and brutal trying to get answers about Teaberry's fate. Broke B'BallStar saw the gumshoe twosome as he paused in mid-jumpshot form and peered over his basketball through the playground fence at the black heavy Chevy mobile fortress Petalstool and Epidural called home.

"What the hell do they want NOW?" Broke mumbled to himself. Epidural blared through the horn to give clarity of the visit.

"Teaberry got slumped and we're looking for the punk or punktress that pulled this stunt."

It's not that the gumshoes cared about the fate of any natives but always had to justify their jobs. Not just their jobs but their very existence as the armed power in a police state that was all too familiar to the natives. As a rule of thumb, the natives never seek the endorsement of law enforcement unless the forces of law contribute to the forces of ghetto sustenance and then and only then, can the po-lice truly be a native's friend. An arrangement, if you will. A place where alleged legitimacy cuts side deals with good and ill willed natives.

Teaberry's life wasn't complicated. A simple brother who played the violin, smoked a lot of weed and bedded a lot of women simply because of his "refined" good looks and charming ways. Who would kill such a ghetto icon in such a nasty fashion in the shadows of palm trees and brownstones in Mystical Brooklyn? Epidural and Petalstool are looking to find out!

The Critic

I see the sisters reading and writing, articulating us without our input.

They write, they say, "I love my brother but
he doesn't know how to love me."

The sisters write, they say, in the name of ART,
"we celebrate LOVE!"
While wondering where the brothers are,
wondering WHY the brothers are…

I see the brothers hanging and rapping, articulating us
without our input.

They write, they rap, "Blast that NIGGER and fuck that BITCH!"

The brothers rap, they say, in the name of ART,
"we pass on HATE."
Dancing like nut-hugging jean wearing thug like a bad scene from
Niggas in Paris is Burning.
Acting like the Notorious B.S.G. (Bull Shit Gangsta)

I hear the babies talking and I listen to them sobbing about us
without our input. They repeat, they parrot,
"Put it in your mouth… licky, licky, sticky, sticky."

The babies see, they observe in the name of ART appreciation:
LIFE imitating
ART imitating
LIFE imitating
ART imitating…

I saw the babies grow into little brothers and sisters in the streets
Growing about us without our input.

They laugh, they play, they sing
"Blast a NIGGER and fuck that BITCH!"

The babies see, they still observe in the name of ART appreciation.

I see an industry pimping the legacy with our input
Poison products promotion poison lyrics and KISS-POWERed
Music TV images talk out the side of their mouths,
They defend, they,
"We ain't raising y'all's kids! We're promoting ART!"
LIFE imitating
ART imitating
LIFE imitating
ART imitating…

I witnessed a brother dying on the street. I saw him bleeding like a
blasted NIGGER living the life of
a Bull Shit Gangsta a.k.a. The Notorious D.O.A.

I heard a sister crying because she had to tell the babies that
Daddy lived a LIFE imitating
ART imitating
LIFE imitating
ART imitating…
DEATH.

Exclusive! Charles Pernell Interviews Fawn of that Wacky demi-god tandem of Dewey and Fawn!

I first met Dewey and Fawn a little over seven years ago as I was transitioning in my own life. I found them sitting on the stoop of an undisclosed Brooklyn brownstone within myself. They had been there all along but I had never met them, at least not directly. A pleasant couple, they continued to greet me with courtesy and warmth every time they passed through my mind. Dewey and Fawn are spectacular entities in that they don't live in the world, but live about it. They move through lives somewhat as specters but always as spectators. They are some of humanity's greatest fans.

We met at a popular coffee shop that had valet parking. I saw them pull up in Dewey's 2007 B.C. Apollo coupe chariot, rimmed out with the most beautiful black stallions to provide the crazy horsepower. Of course the valet attendants were perplexed. Although we were in L.A. at the time and valet parking at Starbucks and TGI Friday's was a norm, chariots were not. Dewey, smiled and said, "I'll park it, thank you." He snapped his fingers, and the chariot and horses vanished. That's the kind of stuff I'm talking about. Always producing the unexpected.

Part 1 of our interview went like this:

Charles: Thank you two for coming and sharing with us. I know this is a big step but this is a great way for the world to get to know you. Fawn, we'll start with you. Tell me a little about yourself.

Fawn: Well, Charles, not much to tell. I think I am a somewhat shy person. I love to run. I run like the wind because I am.

Charles: You "are" what?

Fawn: I am the wind. I am the air you breathe. I move the seas and trees when I run. I never blow time, I just harness it and ride it.

Charles: Um, yeah... tell us about your family background?

Fawn: My upbringing was typical. Growing up in a neighborhood very similar to where Dewey and I stay now. I grew up near the corner of Olympus Parkway and Crenshaw Boulevard in South Central BK. My parents were every day deities. My dad, HeyZeus is a proud and beautiful Latin god who lives in rhythms and beats. He's made a handsome living off of that over the centuries. My mom is Kizzakay. She's a naturalist. Rules nature and the elements. That's why I am Wind. You heard of the Santa Monica Mountains? Me and mommy did that when I was like... well I was pretty young. Pretty normal childhood, I guess.

Charles: What is one of your more valued memories of your youth?

Fawn: I ran in the first Olympics in 776 B.C. That's where I met Dewey. (*Glimpsed over lovingly over at Dewey.*) He was... hawking bootleg DVDs from out the back of chariot up outside of the Coliseum. I mean they were DVDs of the Peloponnesian War although it hadn't even occurred yet. He was kind of a shifty character but I loved him. He was a hustler. I think he was a student at the University at the time? Philosophy major.

Charles: Would you say this was the beginning of your love affair?

Fawn: (*blushes*) I wouldn't say it was the "beginning". We had always loved one another. It is one of the more memorable meetings between the two of us throughout the eons. Dewey is my man. Always was. Always will be.

Charles: Tell me about the Olympics. What was your event and where did you place?

Fawn: I ran the marathon. I won, of course (she smiles). It wasn't that I was so competitive that it drove me to victory. The season premiere of Sponge Bobicus was coming on so I ran all the way home to catch it. The victory tape just happened to be there on my way back the house.

Charles: Quite an enchanting tale. So what do you now for a living or... as an existence I should say?

Fawn: I still run and I'm still the wind. I give those in pain respite. I breathe life and hope into their despair. I refresh them with a breeze of love.

Charles: How do you do that?

Fawn: Well, I can't give up all the tapes today, Charles. Damn. You gonna have to just hang around and see how me and Dewey do? You like that? How me and Dewey do! (she laughs). You need to ask Dewey some questions, man!

End (for now)

ABOUT THE AUTHOR

Camden, NJ native Charles Pernell has been a community activist, part-time newspaper journalist, active blogger, visionary, business owner and a recliner salesman. He acknowledges that writing is his first love. The 25-year Air Force veteran currently resides near Tacoma, WA with his wife and two youngest children.

www.ingramcontent.com/pod-product-compliance
Lightning Source LLC
Chambersburg PA
CBHW070353130626
46556CB00007B/3158